But If They Do

Text by **Bill Richardson**   Illustrations by **Marc Mongeau**

ANNICK PRESS

TORONTO + NEW YORK + VANCOUVER

Nighty night
Sleep tight
Don't let   **The bedbugs bite.**

BUT
IF
THEY
DO—

I'll jump up on a pogo stick
And pogo cross the floor!
I'll drive 'em from the bedroom
With a mighty lion roar!

Roar! Roar!
I'll floor 'em with my roar!
I'll pinch their little bedbug bums
And shoo 'em out the door!

Nighty night
Sleep sound
Don't let **The ghouls come round.**

BUT
IF
THEY
DO–

I'll grab 'em by their pointy horns
And catch 'em by their tails!
I'll take 'em by their nasty claws
And rattle all their scales!

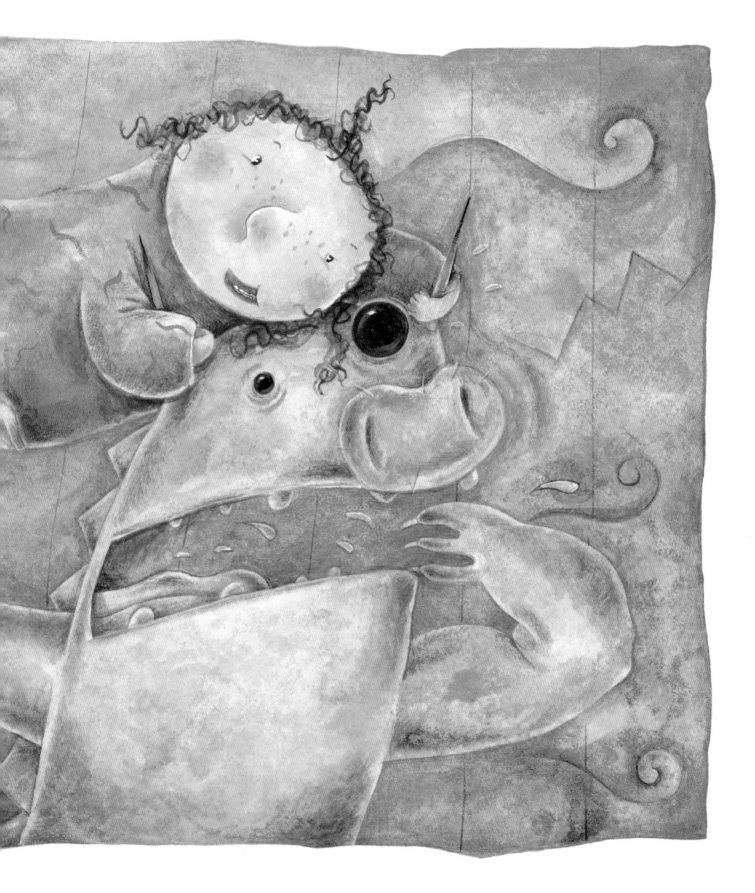

Scales! Scales!
I'll rattle all their scales!
I'll make 'em eat a stinky stew
Of goop and rusty nails!

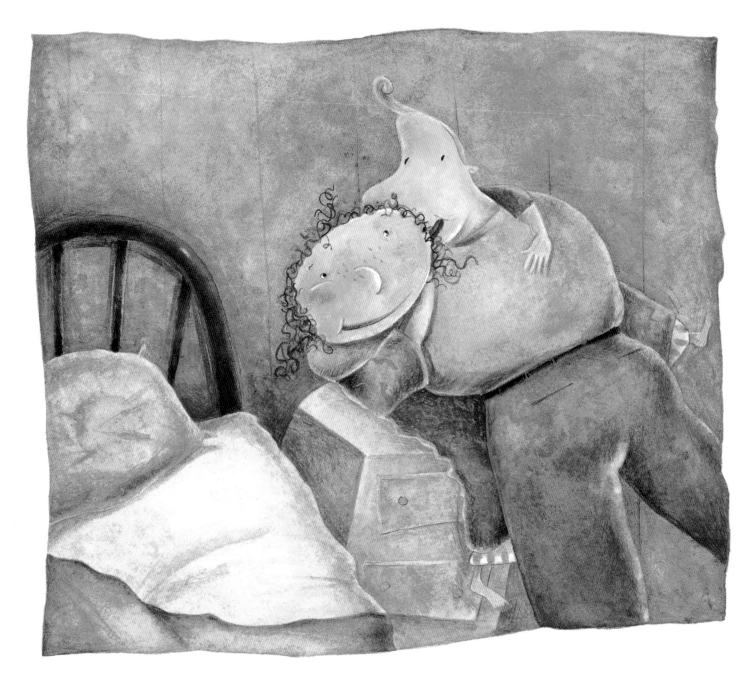

Nighty night
Sweet dreams
Don't let **The monsters scream.**

BUT
IF
THEY
DO–

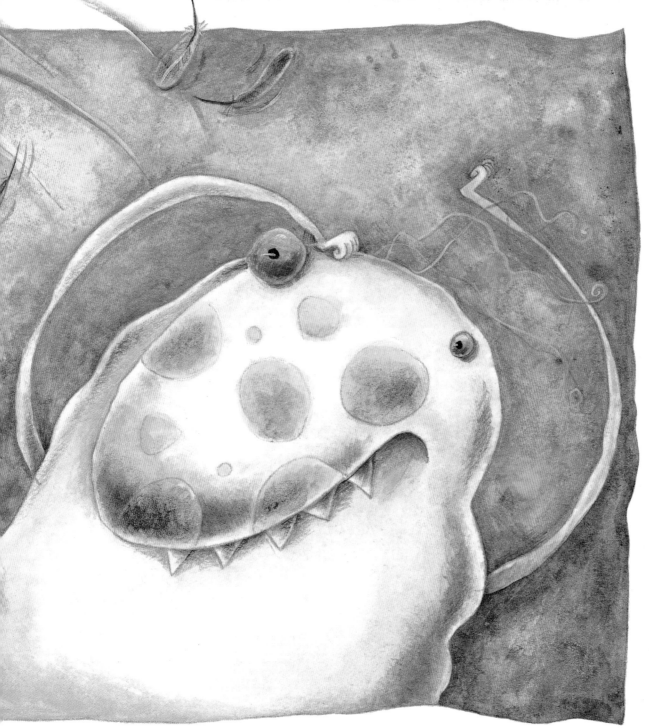

I'll pound 'em in a pillow fight
And beat 'em black and blue!

I'll lock 'em in the closet
And say "Fooey on you!"
Foo! Foo! Fooey on you!
Monsters who hear "fooey"
Hang their heads and cry "Boo-hoo."

Nighty night
Dream deep
Don't let **The vampires creep.**

BUT
IF
THEY
DO—

I'll take my trusty water gun
And give a mighty squirt!
I'll dunk 'em in the garbage can
And cover 'em in dirt!

Dirt! Dirt! I'll cover 'em in dirt!
Then send 'em home to mommy
With a ripped and filthy shirt.

Nighty night   Nighty night
Big hugs   That's that
No ghouls   No monsters
No bugs.   No bats.

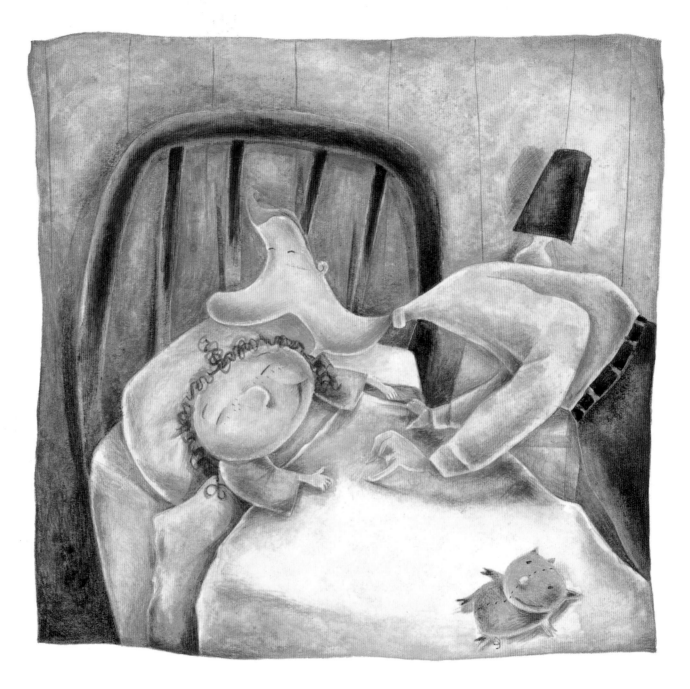

Nighty night
No buts
Sleepy, sleepy
Eyes shut.

Annick Press Ltd.

We acknowledge the support of the Canada Council for the Arts, the Ontario Arts Council, and the Government of Canada through the Book Publishing Industry Development Program (BPIDP) for our publishing activities.

All ideas start somewhere, and this one began on my radio program. People called in to talk about "good night" rhymes, including "Nighty night, sleep tight, don't let the bedbugs bite." Of course I had often heard that charm spoken, but many callers reported that their family tradition was to continue the rhyme by explaining all the dire things that might happen to a biting bug. And that got me thinking. This book is the result.

Designed by Irvin Cheung/iCheung Design

Cataloguing in Publication Data

Richardson, Bill, 1955-
    But if they do / text by Bill Richardson ; illustrations by Marc Mongeau.

ISBN 1-55037-787-6 (bound).--ISBN 1-55037-786-8 (pbk.)

    I. Mongeau, Marc II. Title.

PS8585.I186B88 2003   jC813'.54   C2002-904775-7
PZ7

The art in this book was rendered in watercolor.
The text was typeset in Interstate.

Distributed in Canada by
Firefly Books Ltd.
3680 Victoria Park Avenue
Willowdale, ON
M2H 3K1

Published in the U.S.A. by
Annick Press (U.S.) Ltd.

Distributed in the U.S.A. by
Firefly Books (U.S.) Inc.
P.O. Box 1338
Ellicott Station
Buffalo, NY 14205

Manufactured in China

visit us at **www.annickpress.com**